FRANKIE'S MAGIC FOOTBALL

BY FRANK LAMPARD

FRANKIE'S MAGIC FOOTBALL

FRANKIE VS THE PIRATE PILLAGERS

FRANK LAMPARD

LITTLE, BROWN BOOKS FOR YOUNG READERS
lbkids.co.uk

LITTLE, BROWN BOOKS FOR YOUNG READERS

First published in Great Britain in 2013 by Little, Brown Books
for Young Readers
This paperback edition published in 2015 by Hodder & Stoughton

17 19 20 18

A CIP catalogue record for this book
is available from the British Library.

ISBN 978-0-349-00162-3

Typeset in Cantarell by M Rules
Printed and bound in Great Britain by
Clays Ltd, St Ives plc

The paper and board used in this book are
made from wood from responsible sources.

MIX
Paper from
responsible sources
FSC® C104740

Little, Brown Books for Young Readers
An imprint of
Hachette Children's Group
Part of Hodder & Stoughton
Carmelite House
50 Victoria Embankment
London EC4Y 0DZ

An Hachette UK Company
www.hachette.co.uk

www.lbkids.co.uk

To my mum Pat,
who encouraged me to do my
homework in between kicking a ball
all around the house, and is still
with me every step of the way.

*Welcome to a fantastic
fantasy league – the greatest
football competition ever held in
this world or any other!*

*You'll need four on a team,
so choose carefully. This is a lot
more serious than a game in the
park. You'll never know who your
next opponents will be, or where
you'll face them.*

*So lace up your boots, players,
and good luck! The whistle's
about to blow!*

The Ref

CHAPTER 1

"Shall we go in too?" Frankie asked. "Maybe Lou got lost."

"Nah," said Charlie, darting a glance towards the haunted house. "She'll be out soon."

Frankie and Charlie were standing by the exit, waiting for their friend Louise. The sun was

3

dropping behind the Ferris wheel, and soon the funfair would be shutting down for the year and leaving town.

"Not scared, are you?" said Frankie.

Charlie blushed, and all his freckles stood out. "Course not."

Frankie grinned. He remembered that Charlie hadn't wanted to go in last year either. It *was* pretty scary. There were walking skeletons, dangling spiders and wailing ghosts. He would have gone in again today with Lou, but it cost a pound and he only had fifty pence left.

Frankie's dog Max was looking up hopefully at the stick of candyfloss in Frankie's hand.

"Too sugary for you," Frankie said. He reached into his pocket and pulled out a doggy biscuit. Max opened his mouth and Frankie dropped it in, then tickled the dog under his furry white muzzle.

The doors opened and a few screams drifted over. Then a balding man stumbled out, with pale skin and wide eyes. It was their PE teacher, Mr Donald.

"Looks like Donaldo's spooked," said Frankie.

Mr Donald saw them and walked

over, smoothing down the few hairs on his head.

"Is that a spider on your shoulder, sir?" asked Charlie.

Mr Donald jumped about a foot in the air, craning his neck.

"Only joking, sir," said Charlie.

Mr Donald fixed them with a frown. "I hope to see you both for football practice tomorrow."

"Of course, sir," said Frankie. "We wouldn't miss practice for anything!"

Mr Donald walked off, still checking his shoulder.

The doors of the haunted house creaked open again and Louise emerged. She was playing on her handheld console.

"We thought a skeleton might have got you," said Frankie.

Louise rolled her eyes. "*Sooo* unscary – I almost fell asleep."

Frankie checked his watch and saw it was nearly quarter to five. "We should go home – my mum wants me back by half past five."

"Mine too," said Louise.

They made their way past the dodgems and the coconut shy. Their friend Kobe from school was standing behind a rope, trying to knock the coconuts off their stands with tennis balls.

"Here, Kobe!" said Charlie. "Try me!"

Kobe turned and launched a throw towards Charlie. Charlie dived and caught the ball in his goalie gloves.

Max barked excitedly.

"The best keepers are . . . " Charlie began.

" . . . always ready!" said Frankie and Louise. They'd heard it a gazillion times.

Charlie threw the ball back. He *never* took his gloves off, except when the teachers forced him to. He said he even slept wearing them. Charlie might have been small, but Frankie knew he was the best goalie in their year at school. Probably better than anyone in the year above too.

"Won any prizes, Kobe?" asked Frankie.

His friend shook his head. "Nope. I've hit the coconuts, but they don't fall off. Watch."

He crouched like a baseball pitcher and hurled a ball. It smashed right into a coconut, which didn't even wobble.

"Better luck next time," said the stallholder, a short woman in a woolly hat and thick coat.

"I reckon it's a fix," huffed Kobe.

"Watch what you say, young man," said the stallholder. "I'm as honest as they come. Straight as an arrow."

But Kobe was already hopping over the rope towards the coconuts. He grabbed one and tried to tug it from its holder. "See!" he said. "I knew it — you're cheating!"

"Must be the hot weather," said the stallholder, folding her beefy arms. "It's made the coconuts swell up."

"I don't think coconuts do that," said Frankie.

"Fix!" said Louise.

"Fix!" echoed Charlie, and Max began to bark too.

The stallholder shuffled over and put her fingers to her lips. "Keep it down, will you? Here!" She snatched a large pink teddy bear down from a peg and thrust it towards Kobe. "Take this and go."

Kobe looked at the bear with a frown. "I suppose my sister might like it. See you at school, guys."

As Kobe strolled off with his prize, Frankie and his friends walked towards the exit. The cheating stallholder had left a sour taste in Frankie's mouth. He hated when people didn't play fair.

Behind the hot dog stand, another stall caught his eye. It had a painted sign showed a football whizzing through the air. *How come I didn't notice it earlier?* Frankie wondered.

"Hang on, guys," he said, walking over.

Max lingered for a moment, staring up at some sausages turning on a hotplate.

"Come on, Max," said Frankie. "You'll get your dinner later."

At the football stall, an ancient man with bushy grey hair was up a ladder about to take down the sign.

"Is it too late for a go?" Frankie asked.

The old man shook his head as he climbed down the ladder. "I'm afraid . . . " When he saw Frankie he paused, then nodded. "I suppose one more won't hurt. Fifty pence gets you three shots. Get it in the bucket and you win a prize."

He reached under the counter and pulled out a football. It must have been almost as old as he was. The ball was half flat, and the leather was cracked and peeling off.

He set it down in front of Frankie. Max sniffed at it, then whined.

"That bucket is tiny," said Charlie. "It might be another con job."

Frankie stared at the old man. There was something odd about him, with his eyebrows like bristling caterpillars and his deep wrinkles, but he looked honest enough. Frankie fished his last fifty pence out of his pocket and put it on the counter. He took a step back and drew in a breath. With a stab of his toe, he sent the ball sailing over the top of the bucket.

"Unlucky," said Louise.

The old man placed the ball back at Frankie's feet. "Two goes left."

Frankie looked up at the bucket, trying to fix it in his mind. This time he chipped the ball into the air with

15

less power. He heard his friends all suck in a breath.

The ball dropped towards the bucket, bounced off the rim . . .

. . . and on to the ground.

"Close," said the stallholder, "but not close enough." He fetched the ball back again.

"Told you," said Charlie. "I doubt the ball even fits."

But Frankie didn't like to give up. He closed his eyes and told himself to relax.

"You can do it, Frankie," whispered Louise.

Frankie opened his eyes, took a step, and kicked the ball. It spun as

it rose through the air, then looped
down. It plonked right into the
centre of the bucket.

"SUPERGOOAAALL!"
yelled Frankie, throwing his arms in
the air.

"Great shot!" said Charlie,

clapping him on the back. Max jumped up on his hind legs.

The old man rubbed his chin, his mouth gaping. "Well, I've not seen a chip that good for many a year," he said.

Frankie smiled and blushed.

"What's the prize?" asked Charlie.

The old man looked at his feet. "Erm . . . I don't have one."

"Eh?" said Charlie.

"Well, no one usually wins," he said. He looked Frankie right in the eye and held his gaze. "Tell you what, you can have the ball if you like."

"Oh, great," grumbled Louise. "Even Max won't touch it."

But Frankie nodded. He wasn't sure why, but something drew him to the battered football.

The old man picked the ball out of the bucket and tossed it to them.

Frankie caught it on the arch of his foot and balanced it perfectly. "Must be my lucky ball," he said.

"You never know," said the stallholder, with a twinkle in his eye. "It might just be. Here, you'd better have this back."

The old man flicked the fifty pence over. Before it reached

Frankie, Charlie's hand shot out and caught it. "Always ready," he said.

Frankie laughed. "Come on, let's go."

CHAPTER 2

"Have we got time for a kickabout?" asked Louise, nodding to the park gates opposite the funfair.

Frankie checked his watch. Ten past five. *There's always time for football,* he thought. "Maybe for ten minutes."

They ran into the park. At first,

Frankie thought it was completely empty. Then a voice called out: "Look who it is, Kev!"

Frankie turned around and saw his brother Kevin with two of his friends. They were leaning against a fence, drinking cans of energy drink.

"Cool ball, Frank*enstein*," said Kevin. He laughed at his lame joke, downed his drink, then dropped the can on the grass.

"Let's leave them to it," muttered Charlie.

But Frankie's blood was boiling. "You should put that in the bin, Kev," he said.

"Oh?" said his brother. "You gonna tell Mum?"

Frankie stared at him. He knew full well that if their mum *could* see what Kevin had done, she'd drag him home by his ear.

Frankie walked towards his brother, then stooped to get the can. If Kevin wouldn't put it in the bin, he would. But at the last moment, his brother kicked the can out of reach. "Nice try," he sniggered. Frankie reached again, and Kev dribbled it away, laughing. "Too slow, Frankenstein!" he said.

"That's enough," said Louise.

Kevin lifted his foot to kick the

can away. "Hey!" he shouted, as
Max charged in. The little dog
snapped up the can in his jaws
and ran off. Kevin lost his balance
as he swung his leg and fell on
his backside. Max trotted to a
bin, stood on his hind paws and
dropped the can in.

Frankie managed to keep a
straight face, but Kevin's friends
burst out laughing.

"Great skills!" said one of them.

"Tackled by a dog, man!" said the
other.

Kevin clambered to his feet,
blushing bright red. His jeans had
a dark grass stain on the back and

he turned angrily to Frank. "You'd better not be late for tea!" he said, and stormed off. His friends followed.

"Or what?" Frankie called after him jokingly. "You gonna tell Mum?" He gave Max another treat. "We'd better make this a quick game," he said to the others.

"There!" said Charlie, pointing to a climbing frame shaped like a model ship. He jogged over and stood in front of it. "The ship's the goal."

Frankie booted the ball high into the air. Max streaked after it. It tangled in his feet, and he tumbled over the top.

"Pass it!" called Frankie.

Max managed to nose the ball to Louise. She dribbled the ball in and out of the swings, then sent a curling shot towards the top corner of the goal. Charlie dived and just got his fingertips to the ball.

"Nothing gets past me!" said Charlie.

We'll see about that . . . thought Frankie. He fetched the ball and passed it to Louise. She looked up, ready to shoot, then stepped over the ball and flicked it up with her heel. Frankie was ready. He brought his foot round and connected with a perfect volley. The ball screamed towards the goal. Charlie leapt sideways, gloves splayed, but the ball passed beneath his outstretched hands. Frankie slid on to his knees, thinking his mum would kill him when she saw the grass stains.

"**SUPERGOA...**"

The shout trailed off in Frankie's throat.

The ball had vanished, and so had the model ship. Max growled quietly. Frankie stood up, his heart thumping. He couldn't believe what was before his eyes.

Where the goal had been just a second before was a swirl of light like nothing he'd ever seen. Colours flashed and spun in a disc shape, three metres across. He looked at Louise. Her jaw had dropped open.

Charlie picked himself up, bashing the ground with his fist. He still hadn't seen the spinning circle of light behind him. "I was so close!" he said.

"Er, Charlie," said Louise. "You might want to turn around."

He did as she told him, then leapt backwards. "Holy moly! What is that thing?"

Frankie and Louise joined Charlie's side. The lights shifted and shimmered like oil on water.

"I have no idea!" said Frankie.
"But it must be linked to the ball. I
knew there was something weird
about that stall."

He reached towards the . . .
the . . . whatever it was.

"What are you doing?" asked
Charlie.

Frankie turned to his friend. "My
ball's through there somewhere,"
he said. "I have to get it back."

"Are you crazy?" said Charlie.

Frankie grinned. "It's just like
when it goes into Mrs Pratchett's
garden."

Mrs Pratchett was Frankie's
grumpy next-door neighbour. There
was only one thing she hated more
than slugs in her garden, and that
was Frankie's football.

"This isn't quite the same," said
Charlie.

"Anyway," said Frankie, "it must

31

be my lucky ball. I got it past you, didn't I?"

Charlie started to mumble something about being "lucky" and Frankie stepped closer. He swallowed as his hand passed through the surface of the swirling colours. "It feels warm." He held out his other hand to his friends. "Who's with me?"

"I am!" said Louise at once. She gripped Frankie's hand.

Charlie shook his head. "I hope I don't regret this." He took Louise's hand in his goalie gloved one.

Max nuzzled at Frankie's ankle.

Frankie took another step, and

his arm slipped into nothingness up to the elbow. His skin tingled all over, as if electricity were passing through his whole body. "Now or never," he said.

Something gripped his arm and sucked him in.

CHAPTER 3

"What . . . Wow . . . WHOAH!"

Blackness swallowed Frankie.
He felt his body tossed from side
to side. The others were crying out
in alarm. Louise's fingers clutched
his tightly as he turned upside
down. Colours swirled all around.
Frankie found himself hurtling

down a rainbow-coloured chute
feet first. He'd been on plenty of
roller coasters in his time, but this
was something else. He lost his grip
on Louise as he spun around, head
first, on his back, on his stomach,
on his side. It was like a water slide,
but without any water, and much,
much quicker.

Frankie managed to steady
himself as he looped around a
bend. In a flash he saw the others
shooting along behind him, limbs
flailing.

"Uh oh!" called Louise, her eyes
staring past Frankie.

He turned and faced the way he

was travelling. His heart thumped in panic. Ahead, the tunnel seemed to disappear as it turned downwards. Frankie scrabbled against the walls, but they were more slippery than a wet pitch. He couldn't slow himself down.

"SORREEEEEEEEE!" he cried as he plummeted over the ledge.

The chute was bottomless, and down he tumbled, wind rushing in his hair. Then he saw something. Wooden boards, rushing towards him. *This is it,* he thought, bracing himself. *This is the end . . .*

The impact never came. All was dark, until Frankie realised he had his eyes closed. He was on his back, lying on a hard surface. The world seemed to rock beneath him and something wet touched his face. When he opened his eyes he saw Max's furry face close to his, tongue lolling. Beyond him was a clear blue sky. A flag with a skull and crossbones design flew from a mast. A seagull screeched overhead.

A seagull? But we're nowhere near the sea . . .

Frankie sat up and gasped. He was sitting on the deck of some sort of old ship. The boards and masts were all made of timber.

Complicated ropes trailed from the sails to great coils below. Beyond the rails at the edges of the deck, dark blue water stretched in every direction. A salty smell filled his nostrils.

The others were picking themselves up too, and looking about in wonder. Frankie was glad to see no one was hurt, but they definitely looked worse for wear. Louise was dressed in a black skirt cut off just above her knees and a purple shirt. Charlie wore red shorts, a salt-stained blue jacket and some sort of spotty headscarf. Frankie looked down at himself and saw similar clothing: dirty blue shorts and a stripy sailor's top. He reached to his head and pulled off a crushed velvety hat with gold trim.

"We're at sea!" said Charlie. As he took a step back, there was a crunch, and he looked down. Frankie saw Louise's console under his foot.

"Argh!" cried Louise. She crouched beside him. There was a huge crack across the screen. "It's broken!"

"I didn't mean to," said Charlie.

Louise shook her head. "My dad will go mad. He's always telling me not to take it out of the house."

Frankie put a hand on her shoulder. "It might still work," he said.

Louise pressed a switch on the side of the console. Sparks shot out of the device and she dropped it back on to the deck. "Oh!" she cried.

The console twitched on the boards and the screen glowed. Rays of light shot out of the screen, then spread out into the hologram of a man. He wore a tight-fitting black T-shirt and shorts like a football referee. A whistle dangled around his neck. He turned to Frankie, and his image flickered.

"Greetings!" he said. "Welcome to the fantasy league. State team name . . . "

"What?" said Frankie. He thought the man looked familiar.

The referee checked his watch. "No time for warming up. You have been selected to play in the fantasy league. A team name, please."

"Frankie's FC!" said Louise.

"Hang on . . . " said Frankie.

"Your ball, your team," said Charlie.

"So be it," said the Ref. Frankie felt a slight buzzing on his chest. When he looked down, an emblem had appeared there, with "FFC" written in an upside down triangle.

"Cool!" he muttered.

"Frankie's FC," said the Ref. "You have been drawn to play the Pirate Pillagers."

"Pirates?" said Frankie. So that's what the skull and crossbones meant.

"Right ye are, me hearties," said a voice.

Frankie and his friends spun around. A man wearing a tattered red jacket stood before them. In the place of one of his legs was a wooden peg. His straggly brown hair looked like it needed a good wash and he had a thick coating of stubble on his chin. At his side he wore a cutlass.

"Who are you?" asked Louise.

The pirate limped forwards, his wooden leg knocking on the deck. Frankie noticed that the buttons on his jacket were the shape of miniature footballs. "I be Captain Cropper, owner of this vessel, *The Jolly Striker*, and I think ye stowaways have come to steal my treasure."

"Actually, we just came to get our ball back," said Charlie.

The captain scowled. "Yer ball, ye say! Well, what about *that*, Rolf?"

The deck creaked as a huge man emerged wearing an open leather jerkin. He must have been seven feet tall, with tattoos covering his barrel chest and a hook for a hand. In his other hand, he gripped the magic football. "Looking for this, are ye?"

Frankie gulped and nodded.

A flash of colour caught his eye, and a parrot with red and yellow wings and a blue breast landed on the ship's wheel. It opened its beak and squawked, "This'll be easy! They're just kids."

"Did that bird just talk?" said Charlie.

"What's so weird about that?" said a gruff voice at Frankie's feet.

He looked down and saw Max staring at him.

"Did you just . . . "

"Sure did," said Max.

Frankie was still goggling at his pet dog when a figure came swinging down on a rope. It was a girl, perhaps a year older than them, with bright red hair and baggy turquoise trousers. She landed lightly on the deck and bowed low to Frankie. "Scarlet's the name, and this 'ere parrot is Tito."

Captain Cropper sneered, revealing a couple of gold teeth. "So, landlubbers! Ready to face finest team on the seven seas?"

CHAPTER 4

Louise laughed, then tried to cover it with her hand.

"Something funny, missy?" asked the captain.

"I just didn't know pirates played football," Louise replied.

Rolf growled and chucked the ball into the air. Tito the parrot swooped down and knocked it with his beak to Scarlet. She flipped on to her hands, caught the ball between her feet and tossed it to Captain Cropper. He bounced the ball on one foot three times then pinned it against the deck with his wooden leg.

"Yer in for a surprise, missy," he said.

"What's the prize?" asked Charlie. "And don't say buried treasure!"

The Ref flickered above Louise's console. "The winner will get to play again."

"And the loser?" gulped Frankie.

Rolf extended his hooked hand

over the side of the ship. "The loser ends up there — until they build a raft or the crabs eat 'em!"

Frankie squinted and saw a low, flat island, dotted with palm trees and not much else. *It's my fault we're here*, he thought. *There's no way I'm letting my friends get marooned on a desert island!*

"May the best dog win!" said Max, scampering back and forth.

Frankie swelled his chest and stepped up to face Captain Cropper. He held out his hand. "Let's start the game!"

Captain Cropper snarled at the hand.

"Where's the goal?" said Charlie. "Shall we use a couple of masts?"

The Ref shook his head. "Each game in the league has different rules."

Scarlet drew her cutlass and pointed to a tiny basket on top of the main mast. "The winner is the first to score three goals in the crow's nest."

"That's not how we play back home," said Louise.

"Not our problem," said Captain Cropper, throwing the ball on to the centre of the deck. As soon as it stopped, a cannon blasted from the side of the ship, making Frankie's ears ring.

"Ready?" said the Ref. He brought his whistle to his lips and blew.

Captain Cropper pounced towards the ball and Frankie dashed in too. He slid across the deck and reached the ball first, sending it between his opponent's legs. Frankie scooped the ball on to his foot and sent it curling into the crow's nest.

"Barnacles!" muttered the Captain.

"One-nil to Frankie's team!" shouted Charlie.

"Beginner's luck!" squawked
Tito.

The game restarted with another
boom from the cannon, and again
Frankie closed on the ball first. He
barely heard Louise call "Look out!"
before Rolf ploughed into him.
Frankie went tumbling across the
deck like a toppled skittle.

"That's a foul!" said Louise.
"Ref?"

But the Ref seemed to have
disappeared.

Rolf grinned at Frankie. "Nothing
wrong with a little shoulder barge."

Max ran at the huge pirate, but
bounced off his leg.

We might as well try to tackle an oak tree! thought Frankie.

Rolf kicked the ball to Scarlet. With a swish of a leg, she chipped the ball into the crow's nest.

"One a piece!" said Scarlet.

"What are we going to do?" Charlie said.

Max's ears pricked up. "We need to stop chasing our tails."

Charlie rubbed his forehead with a gloved hand. "I can't believe I'm taking advice from a dog."

As the cannon sounded, Frankie sprinted towards the ball. Rolf charged in again, but Frankie stalled, then stepped nimbly past

him. Cropper was closing in, so
Frankie passed the ball to Louise.
As she steadied herself to shoot,
Scarlet came swinging down on
a rope. Louise looked up, and
bounced the ball off the bottom of
a mast. It rolled to Max's feet.

"Shoot!" yelled Charlie.

"Knock it in!" called Louise.

Max took a few steps back, spun
on the spot and kicked the ball
with his back legs. It bounced off
a barrel and flew up towards the
crow's nest. He wagged his stubby
tail in triumph.

It's going in . . . thought Frankie.
He's done it!

Just as the ball hovered over the goal, Tito flapped into view and batted it with his wing.

The ball spun over the edge of the ship and landed with a splash.

"Drat and cats!" barked Max.

Everyone ran to the deck rail.

"Our throw-in," said Louise.

Frankie saw the water churning with dozens of triangular fins. "Sharks!" he said. One of the deadly creatures broke the surface of the water, jagged teeth bared.

"If they eat the ball, we can't get home!" said Charlie.

But instead of swallowing the ball, the shark nosed it out of the

water. Another one batted it into
the air. A third thumped the ball
with its tail.

"I guess sharks like football too!"
said Frankie.

"Either that, or they don't like the
taste of leather," said Charlie.

After passing it between themselves, one of the sharks flicked the ball back towards the deck, over their heads. It stopped in mid-air, right on Rolf's hooked hand.

"Handball!" yelled Frankie.

"It's not my hand," Rolf leered. Drawing back his arm, he tossed the ball into the crow's nest. "Two-one to the Pillagers!"

CHAPTER 5

Frankie's team gathered around him. "They're better than they look," he said.

"I feel seasick," said Charlie.

"They're nothing but cheats, fouling all the time!" said Louise. "Where's the Ref gone?"

Frankie glanced round. The Ref

was lying in a hammock strung from the mast. He seemed to be asleep.

"I don't think we'll get much help from him," Frankie said. Behind the hammock, the island looked closer than before, but no more inviting. How long could they last there with no food or water?

"Perhaps if we had a better goalie, we wouldn't be losing," muttered Max.

"There aren't even any goalposts!" said Charlie.

"Enough!" said Frankie. He hated seeing his teammates arguing with each other. "We're going to lose unless we play as a team."

"Frankie's right," said Louise. "I don't plan to lose to a bunch of smelly pirates."

"Maybe we need to cheat too," said Max. "I could always give one of them a little nip on the ankle — slow them down, y'know."

"No!" said Frankie.

"I'm just saying," said Max, "it might even up the odds a bit."

"We're not going to stoop to their level," said Frankie. "We play fair."

He peered over his shoulder. Captain Cropper had his foot up on the deck-rail, doing stretches. He flashed Frankie a wide grin. Rolf was showing Scarlet the tattoos on his bulging arms, while Tito stabbed at what looked like a biscuit with his beak.

I bet they've never lost before, thought Frankie. *That's their weakness. They're over-confident.*

"Look, team," he said. "Remember what Donaldo says when we play away from home?"

"Take off those gloves on the bus?" said Charlie.

No one laughed apart from Max, who gave a doggy chuckle.

"Not that," said Frankie. "He says, 'The pitch might look

different, but the game's the same.'"

"This pitch looks *very* different," said Louise. "How can we even score? They've got a flying goalie!"

"I might not be able to fly," said Charlie, "but I'm not useless!"

Frankie huddled closer, and patted his pocket. "We need to distract Tito," he said. "And I've got just the thing." The others listened closely as he explained.

"It's worth a try," said Louise.

"Get a move on!" bellowed Captain Cropper. "I've seen sea-slugs move quicker than you lot!"

They turned to face the Pillagers.

Rolf, Tito and Scarlet had lined up behind their captain. Cropper hooked his thumbs in his belt. "About time," he said. "Decided which one ye'll eat first on the island?" He pointed to Frankie's dog. "That fella looks tasty."

"Don't count your treasure before it's dug up," growled Max.

The cannon fired and a gust of wind sent the smoke drifting back across the deck. Frankie coughed and wiped his stinging eyes, then ran at the ball. He saw the shape of Rolf closing in, so he slid the ball to Louise. She looked up to the crow's nest, as if she was going to shoot.

Tito shot up from the deck and hovered, ready to stop the shot.

Frankie fished one of Max's biscuits out of his pocket and hurled it in the air. The parrot twisted mid-flight and swooped towards the dog treat.

"Now!" said Frankie.

As Tito snapped up the treat, Louise chipped the ball into the crow's nest.

"Two all!" Max barked.

The Ref suddenly sat up. "What . . . Where . . . Oh. Two a piece, is it? Then the next goal wins it." He shut his eyes and began to snore again.

"Oops!" said Tito, landing on the
rigging.

Captain Cropper stamped his
wooden leg on the deck in anger.
"Birdbrain!" he growled. "I'll
pluck you bare if you fall for that
again."

"You said this would be easy," said Scarlet.

The captain narrowed his eyes and a smile spread across his lips. "Time for a change of course," he said.

Scarlet sniggered and Rolf grinned, showing his black, rotting teeth.

Scarlet grabbed a rope, and the captain was creeping closer to the mast. Rolf stamped towards the ship's wheel. *What are they planning?* Frankie wondered.

He looked across to his teammates. "Be ready," he said. "They're up to something."

Louise nodded and her eyes darted across the ship suspiciously.

"Where's Charlie gone?" snapped Max.

Frankie shrugged. He couldn't see Charlie anywhere.

The cannon went off. For some reason, Captain Cropper didn't even move from the mast. He simply raised his hand. Frankie ran for the ball. He was almost there when Captain Cropper lowered his arm and gripped the mast. Rolf swung the wheel violently around and the ship lurched in the water. Frankie lost his balance and tripped. He saw Louise and Max go sprawling too.

As he regained his footing, Frankie saw Captain Cropper casually line up the ball. He gave Frankie sly wink. "Bad luck, kiddies," he said, and kicked the ball perfectly.

Frankie stared in horror as it arced up towards the crow's nest.

It's all over . . .

CHAPTER 6

Frankie saw a shadow behind the sail, near the top of the mast. It was too big to be Tito.

Then a gloved hand reached out and batted the ball away.

"Go, Charlie!" yelled Louise.

Charlie waved, then lost his grip. He slid down the mast like it was a fireman's pole.

The ball landed on the deck and rolled to Max's feet.

"Tackle that mutt!" bellowed Captain Cropper.

Rolf thundered across the deck like a charging bull. The timbers shook under Frankie's feet.

"Shoot!" called Louise.

But Max looked terrified, frozen to the spot as Rolf bore down on him.

He's going to get squashed flat! thought Frankie.

Just as Rolf was about to crash into him, Max scampered to the side. The massive pirate careered into a barrel and went toppling over the top. Max rolled the ball to Louise, but not hard enough. Scarlet and Louise reached it at the same time, and the ball went spinning through the air. It landed right beside Captain Cropper. Frankie was already running. He tipped the ball between the captain's legs, then took aim at the crow's nest.

I'll only get one chance, he thought. *Better not waste it.*

"Look out!" called Louise.

Frankie glanced up. Rolf was running at him, an enormous barrel raised over his head. His eyes were wild with rage and the deck creaked and groaned.

Uh oh, thought Frankie. *I can score, but I'll get flattened!*

He looked left and right, then saw his chance. He fired the ball hard at a winch coiled with rope. With a clunk, the rope began to unfurl and one of the large sails dropped. Rolf was almost on him when the sail dropped over his head.

Frankie heard an "uh" then a mighty crash as the pirate tripped and hit the deck. The sail thrashed as Rolf cursed and writhed beneath it.

"Tito!" bellowed Captain Cropper. "Stop the ball!"

The parrot ruffled his feathers. "You called me birdbrain," he said sulkily.

Frankie imagined he was back at the funfair with nothing more than fifty pence at stake.

He lifted his foot and swung. The wind caught the ball and it wobbled for a moment at the top of its arc. Scarlet tried to swing on a rope to stop it, but Max gripped the other end in his teeth. The ball rolled around the edge of the crow's nest then fell in.

"SUPERGOOAAALLL!"

Captain Cropper groaned and slumped on to the deck.

Frankie's teammates piled on top of him, cheering.

"We won!" said Louise.

"Three-two!" said Charlie.

"I never doubted us!" Max yapped.

A loud whistle cut through the air.

As Frankie pulled himself free, he saw the Ref standing over the ball.

"Frankie's FC are the victors," he said. "I've not seen a chip like that for many a year."

His words made Frankie pause. "I knew you looked familiar," he said. "You're the man from the fair!"

The Ref winked. "I've been

looking for a new team," he said.
"Looks like I found one."

With a grinding sound, the
ship suddenly shook from deep in
its belly, and leaned to one side.
Frankie only just managed to keep
his balance.

Rolf peered out from beneath the
tangled sail. "We've run aground!"
he said.

"You're marooned!" said the Ref.
"Just as you requested."

"But . . . but . . . " stuttered
Captain Cropper.

"Don't be sore losers," said
Louise. "Now how do we get home?"

The Ref pointed across the deck,

where a board jutted out over the
water. "Time to abandon ship," he
said.

"You mean walk the plank?" said
Frankie. He peered over the side.
The water looked a long way down.
And what about the sharks?

"Trust me," said the Ref.

"We haven't got much choice,"
said Frankie.

He edged along the plank with
Louise and the others behind
him. When they were all standing
side by side, he grinned at them.
"Ready?"

"Yep!" said Louise.

"Maybe," said Charlie.

"No," said Max. "I hate baths, remember?"

"Until next time," said the Ref.

Frankie leapt off the plank and felt gravity pull him down. He waited for the splash . . .

Instead he found himself sliding across grass on his knees.

" . . . GOOOAAAL!"

The ball bounced off the model ship beneath Charlie's outstretched arm.

The sun was still above the trees. The park was still empty. Louise was sitting on the ground, and Max was rolling over the grass, itching his back.

"Did anyone else just have the strangest dream?" asked Frankie. He looked down at himself and saw his normal clothes and trainers.

Charlie picked up the ball and inspected it. "Er . . . sort of."

Louise held her console in front of her. "Thank goodness for that! It's not broken any more."

Frankie looked at his pet dog. "Max?"

Max cocked his head, wagged his tail, but didn't say anything.

Frankie noticed something gleaming on the ground beside him. *My fifty pence . . .* But when he

picked it up, it was way too heavy.
And it wasn't silver — it was gold!

A gold coin? Pirate treasure!

"Definitely not a dream," said
Louise, peering over Frankie's
shoulder.

"And definitely not the last time
we play in the fantasy league!" said
Frankie.

ACKNOWLEDGEMENTS

Many thanks to Samantha Smith, Charlie King, Kate Webster, Madeleine Feeny and everyone at Little, Brown; Neil Blair, Zoe King, Daniel Teweles and all at The Blair Partnership; Mike Jackson for bringing my characters to life; special thanks to Michael Ford for all his wisdom and patience; and to Steve Kutner for being a great friend and for all his help and guidance not just with this book but with everything.

FRANKIE'S MAGIC FOOTBALL
WEBSITE

Have you had a chance to check out **frankiesmagicfootball.com** yet?

Get involved in **competitions**, find out **news** and **updates** about the series, play **games** and watch **videos** featuring the author, **Frank Lampard!**

Visit the site to join
Frankie's FC today!